W9-DGP-419

THE *Three Wishes*

THE *Three Wishes*

Retold by M. JEAN CRAIG
Pictures by ROSALIND FRY

SCHOLASTIC BOOK SERVICES

NEW YORK • TORONTO • LONDON • AUCKLAND • SYDNEY

This book is sold subject to the condition that it shall not be resold,
lent, or otherwise circulated in any binding or cover other than that
in which it is published—unless prior written permission has been ob-
tained from the publisher—and without a similar condition, including
this condition, being imposed on the subsequent purchaser.

ISBN: 0-590-01621-0

Text copyright © 1968 by M. Jean Craig. Illustrations copyright © 1968 by Rosalind Fry. All
rights reserved. Published by Scholastic Book Services, a division of Scholastic Magazines, Inc.

13 12 11 10 9 8   2 3 4 5 6/8

Printed in the U.S.A.   07

Once upon a time,
a long, long time ago,
there was a poor wood-cutter.
He lived with his wife in a little hut
near the great forest.

Every day the wood-cutter went
into the forest to work.
He took with him his sharp axe.
And he took a bottle of cold tea
and a bag of bread for his lunch.

The wood-cutter worked very hard,
every day of the week.
But he stayed very poor.
And he was tired of being poor.

"I never have anything I want,"
the wood-cutter said.
"I wish I had a warm coat.
I wish we had a bigger house."

"I wish I had a little cart to carry the wood," the wood-cutter said.

"I wish we could eat roast beef sometimes, and apple pie."

But the wood-cutter's wishes did not come true.

One morning when the wood-cutter
was looking for wood, he saw a big oak tree.
He was very pleased.
"What a lot of wood for me!" he said.
"First I will cut it down.
Then I will cut it up!"

He put his bottle of cold tea on the ground.

He put his bag of bread on the ground.

He swung his sharp axe high over his head.

"Oh, don't!" he heard someone say behind him.

The wood-cutter turned and saw...

a tree fairy!

The wood-cutter had never seen a tree fairy before.

His knees began to shake.

His hands began to shake.

His axe fell to the ground with a thump.

"That is my tree! Please don't cut it down!"
cried the tree fairy.
The wood-cutter was so frightened
he could not say a word.

"Please don't cut down my tree,"
begged the tree fairy.
Her eyes were full of tears.

The wood-cutter tried hard to speak.

"Well—" he began.

"Well—" he began again.

"Well, all right, I won't," he said at last.

"I won't cut your tree down if you don't want me to."

"Oh, thank you!" said the tree fairy. "How kind you are!
And now I will do something for you.
I will give you three wishes.
No matter what in the world you wish for,
your next three wishes will come true."
Then the tree fairy was gone.

The wood-cutter picked up his axe and ran
all the way home.

He told his wife about the tree
and the tree fairy.
"We can wish for a real house,
with many windows," said the wood-cutter.

"Or even a tall castle!" said his wife.

"We can wish for a cart, and a goat to pull it,"
said the wood-cutter.

"Or even a shining carriage, with white horses!"
said his wife.

"We can wish for fine new clothes,"
said the wood-cutter.

"Or even strings of pearls and ruby rings!"
said his wife. "We can wish for anything we want!"

"We must think hard before we wish,"
said the wood-cutter.

"Yes, we must be sure to make good wishes,"
said his wife.

They talked for a long time.
They thought of many wishes.

At last the wood-cutter grew hungry.
He was sorry he had left his bag of bread
and his bottle of tea in the forest.
"Is supper ready yet?" he asked.

"Of course not," said the wood-cutter's wife.
"It is much too early for supper."

"Will it be ready soon?" asked the wood-cutter.

"Supper will be ready when it is time for supper,"
said his wife.

"Yes, I know," said the wood-cutter.
"But I am hungry now.
I wish I had a nice piece of sausage right now."

Clatter-bump! Clatter-bang!
A loud noise came from the chimney.
And down fell a great long piece of sausage,
onto the floor.

"Oh, what a fool you are!"
shouted the wood-cutter's wife.
"You have wasted a wish!"

"Oh dear," said the wood-cutter. "So I have."

"You could have wished for a whole pig!"
said the wood-cutter's wife.
"You could have wished for a whole farm,
with a hundred pigs! Only a fool would wish
for just one sausage!"

"You are right. You are right. I am sorry,"
said the wood-cutter.

"You could have wished for a golden crown!
You could have wished for a whole barrel of gold!
And you wished for a sausage!"

"I know," the wood-cutter said.
"I am really very sorry," the wood-cutter said.

The wood-cutter's wife scolded and scolded.

Soon the wood-cutter put his hands over his ears.

"Please stop!" he said.

But the wood-cutter's wife would not stop.

"A sausage!

A sausage!

A sausage!" she shouted, over and over again.

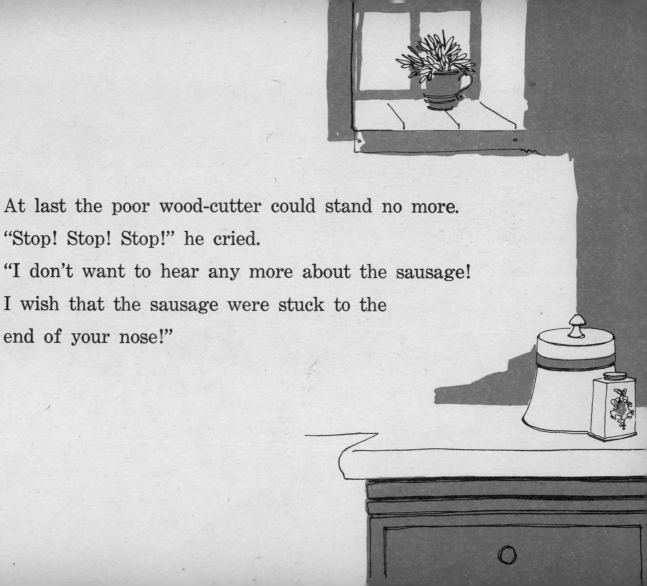

At last the poor wood-cutter could stand no more.

"Stop! Stop! Stop!" he cried.

"I don't want to hear any more about the sausage!

I wish that the sausage were stuck to the

end of your nose!"

And it was.

The great long piece of sausage was stuck to the end

of the wood-cutter's

wife's

nose.

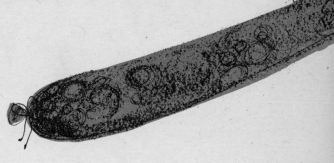

The wood-cutter's wife pulled on the sausage.

It did not come off.

The wood-cutter pulled on the sausage.

It stayed where it was.

The wood-cutter and his wife pulled together.

They pulled until they were tired.

Pulling did no good at all.
The great long piece of sausage
was still stuck to the end
    of the wood-cutter's
      wife's
      nose.

"Do something!"
said the wood-cutter's wife.
"You have one wish left."

The wood-cutter looked hard
at his wife's nose.

"It is not so very bad," he said.

"I could get used to it," he said.

"If we had a whole barrel of gold,
I think I could get used to it," he said.

"But I am sure that I could not!"
cried the wood-cutter's wife.

And so the wood-cutter had to use his last wish.
"I wish that the sausage would come off
the end of your nose," the wood-cutter said.

Plop!

The great long piece of sausage fell from the end
of the wood-cutter's
wife's
nose.

It landed in a white dish that was on the table.

The wood-cutter looked at the sausage.

The wood-cutter's wife looked at the sausage.

"It's time for supper now," she said.

"We might as well eat the sausage right away."

And that is what they did.